With gratitude and respect I dedicate this special edition of Beauty and the Beast
to the people whose dream made the entire "Once Upon A Time" collection
a reality. Their unique vision continues to inspire me.

Tom Peterson   15 March 2000

Illustrations © 1984 Etienne Delessert
Published in 2000 by Creative Editions
123 South Broad Street, Mankato, MN 56001 USA
Creative Editions is an imprint of The Creative Company
Designed by Rita Marshall

All rights reserved. No part of the contents of this book may be reproduced
by any means without the written permission of the publisher.

Printed in Italy
Library of Congress Cataloging-in-Publication Data
Aulnoy, Madame d' (Marie-Catherine), 1650 or 51–1705.
Beauty and the Beast / by Madame d'Aulnoy; illustrated by Etienne Delessert.
Summary: Through her great capacity to love, a kind and beautiful maid
releases a handsome prince from the spell which has made him an ugly beast.
ISBN 1-56846-129-1
[1. Fairy tales. 2. Folklore—France.] I. Delessert, Etienne, ill.
II. Beauty and the beast. English. III. Title.
PZ8.A924Be   2000   398.2'0944'02—dc21   99-29992

First Edition   5 4 3 2 1

BEAUTY AND THE BEAST

A CREATIVE TALE

FROM THE COLLECTION

ONCE UPON A TIME

BY MADAME D'AULNOY

WITH ILLUSTRATIONS BY

ETIENNE DELESSERT

CREATIVE EDITIONS
MANKATO

Pour Rita, la Belle

In a very far-off country, there lived a merchant who had been so fortunate in all his undertakings that he was enormously rich. Even though he had six sons and six daughters, he found that his money was enough to let them all have everything they fancied, as they were accustomed to do.

But one day a most unexpected misfortune befell them. Their house caught fire and was speedily burnt to the ground, with all the splendid furniture, the books, pictures, gold, silver, and precious goods it contained. And this was only the beginning of their troubles. Their father, who had until this moment prospered in all ways, suddenly lost every ship he had upon the sea, either by dint of pirates, shipwreck, or fire. Then he heard that his clerks in distant countries, whom he trusted entirely, had proved unfaithful; and at last from great wealth he fell into the direst poverty.

All that he had left was a little house in a desolate place at least a hundred leagues from the town in which he had lived, and to this he was forced to retreat with his children, who were in despair at the idea of leading such a different life. Indeed, the daughters at first hoped that their friends, who had been so numerous while they were rich, would insist on their staying in their houses now they no longer possessed one. But they soon found that they were left alone, and that their former friends even attributed their misfortunes to their own extravagance, and showed no intention of offering them any help.

So nothing was left for them but to take their departure to the cottage, which stood in the midst of a dark forest and seemed to be the most dismal place upon the face of the earth.

As they were too poor to have any servants, the girls had to work hard, like peasants, and the sons, for their part, cultivated the fields to earn their living. Roughly clothed, and living in the simplest way, the girls regretted unceasingly the luxuries and amusements of their former life. Only the youngest tried to be brave and cheerful. She had been as sad as anyone when misfortune first overtook her father, but, soon recovering her natural gaiety, she set to work to make the best of things, to amuse her father and brothers as well as she could, and to try to persuade her sisters to join her in dancing and singing. But they would do nothing of the sort, and because she was not as doleful as themselves, they declared that this miserable life was all she was fit for. But she was really far prettier and cleverer than they were. Indeed, she was so lovely that she was always called Beauty.

After two years, when they were all beginning to get used to their new life, something happened to disturb their tranquillity. Their father received the news that one of his ships, which he had believed to be lost, had come safely into port with a rich cargo. All the sons and daughters at once thought that their poverty was at an end and wanted to set out directly for the town. But their father, who was more prudent, begged them to wait a little, and, though it was harvest time and he could ill be spared, determined to go himself first, to make inquiries. Only the youngest daughter had any doubt that they would soon again be as rich as they were before, or at least rich enough to live comfortably in some town where they would find amusement and companions once more. So they all loaded their father with commissions for jewels and dresses which it would have taken a fortune to buy. Only Beauty, feeling sure that it was of no use, did not ask for anything. Her father, noticing her silence, said:

"And what shall I bring for you, Beauty?"

"The only thing I wish for is to see you come home safely," she answered.

But this reply vexed her sisters, who fancied she was blaming them for having asked for such costly things. Her father, however, was pleased, but as he thought that at her age she certainly ought to like pretty presents, he told her to choose something.

"Well, dear father," she said, "as you insist upon it, I beg that you will bring me a rose. I have not seen one since we came here, and I love them so much."

So the merchant set out and reached the town as quickly as possible, only to find that his former companions, believing him to be dead, had divided between them the goods which the ship had brought. After six months of trouble and expense, he found himself as poor as when he started, having been able to recover only just enough to pay the cost of his journey. To make matters worse, he was obliged to leave the town in the most terrible weather, so that by the time he was within a few leagues of his home he was almost exhausted with cold and fatigue. Though he knew it would take some hours to get through the forest, he was so anxious to be at his journey's end that he resolved to go on. But night overtook him, and the deep snow and bitter frost made it impossible for his horse to carry him any further. Not a house was to be seen; the only shelter he could get was the hollow trunk of a great tree, and there he crouched all the night, which seemed to him the longest he had ever known. In spite of his weariness, the howling of the wolves kept him awake, and even when at last the day broke, he was not much better off, for the falling snow had covered up every path, and he did not know which way to turn.

At length he made out some sort of track, and, though at the beginning it was so rough and slippery that he fell down more than once, it presently became easier and led him into an avenue of trees which ended in a splendid castle.

It seemed to the merchant very strange that no snow had fallen in the avenue, which was entirely composed of orange trees covered with flowers and fruit. When he reached the first court of the castle, he saw before him a flight of agate steps; he went up them and passed through several splendidly furnished rooms. The pleasant warmth of the air revived him, and he felt very hungry, but there seemed to be nobody in all this vast and splendid palace whom he could ask to give him something to eat. Deep silence reigned everywhere. At last, tired of roaming through empty rooms and galleries, he stopped in a room smaller than the rest, where a clear fire was burning and a couch was drawn up cozily close to it. Thinking that this must be prepared for someone who was expected, he sat down to wait till this person should come, and then very soon fell into a sweet sleep.

When his extreme hunger wakened him after several hours, he was still alone, but a little table, upon which was a good dinner, had been drawn up close to him. As he had eaten nothing for twenty-four hours, he lost no time in beginning his meal, hoping that he might soon have an opportunity of thanking his considerate entertainer, whoever it might be. But no one appeared, and even after another long sleep, from which he awoke completely refreshed, there was no sign of anybody, though a fresh meal of dainty cakes and fruit was prepared upon the little table at his elbow. Being naturally timid, he was terrified by the silence, and he resolved to search once more through all the rooms. But it was of no use. Not even a servant was to be seen. There was no sign of life in the palace!

He began to wonder what he should do, and he amused himself by pretending that all the treasures he saw were his own and considering how he would divide them among his children. Then he went down into the garden, and though it was winter everywhere else, here the sun shone, and the birds sang, and the flowers bloomed, and the air was soft and sweet. The merchant, in ecstasy with all he saw and heard, said to himself:

"All this must be meant for me. I will go this minute and bring my children to share all these delights."

In spite of being so cold and weary when he reached the castle, he had taken his horse to the stable and fed it. Now he thought he would saddle it for his homeward journey, and he turned down the path which led to the stable. This path had a hedge of roses on each side of it, and the merchant thought he had never seen or smelt such exquisite flowers. They reminded him of his promise to Beauty, and he stopped and had just gathered one to take to her when he was startled by a strange noise behind him. Turning round, he saw a frightful Beast, which seemed to be very angry and said in a terrible voice:

"Who told you that you might gather my roses? Was it not enough that I allowed you to be in my palace and was kind to you? This is the way you show your gratitude, by stealing my flowers! But your insolence shall not go unpunished."

The merchant, terrified by these furious words, dropped the fatal rose and, throwing himself on his knees, cried out:

"Pardon me, noble sir. I am truly grateful to you for your hospitality, which was so magnificent that I could not imagine that you would be offended by my taking such a little thing as a rose."

But the Beast's anger was not lessened by this speech.

"You are very ready with excuses and flattery," he cried; "but that will not save you from the death you deserve."

"Alas!" thought the merchant, "if my daughter Beauty could only know what danger her rose has brought me!"

And in despair he began to tell the Beast all his misfortunes and the reason of his journey, not forgetting to mention Beauty's request.

"A king's ransom would hardly have procured all that my other daughters asked," he said, "but I thought that I might at least take Beauty her rose. I beg you to forgive me, for you see I meant no harm."

The Beast considered for a moment, and then he said, in a less furious tone:

"I will forgive you on one condition—that is, that you will give me one of your daughters."

"Ah!" cried the merchant. "If I were cruel enough to buy my own life at the expense of one of my children's, what excuse could I invent to bring her here?"

"No excuse would be necessary," answered the Beast. "If she comes at all, she must come willingly. On no other condition will I have her. See if any one of them is courageous enough and loves you well enough to come and save your life. You seem to be an honest man, so I will trust you to go home. I give you a month to see if one of your daughters will come back with you and stay here, to let you go free. If none of them is willing, you must come alone, after bidding them good-bye forever, for then you will belong to me. And do not imagine that you can hide from me, for if you fail to keep your word, I will come and fetch you!" added the Beast grimly.

The merchant accepted this proposal, though he did not really think any of his daughters would be persuaded to come. He promised to return at the time appointed, and then, anxious to escape from the presence of the Beast, he asked permission to set off at once. But the Beast answered that he could not go until the next day.

"Then you will find a horse ready for you," he said. "Now go and eat your supper and await my orders."

The poor merchant, more dead than alive, went back to his room where the most delicious supper was already served on the little table which was drawn up before a blazing fire. But he was too terrified to eat and only tasted a few of the dishes, for fear the Beast should be angry if he did not obey his orders. When he had finished, he heard a great noise in the next room, which he knew meant that the Beast was coming. As he could do nothing to escape the Beast's visit, the only thing that remained was to seem as little afraid as possible. When the Beast appeared and asked roughly if he had supped well, the merchant answered humbly that he had, thanks to his host's kindness. Then the Beast warned him to remember their agreement and to prepare his daughter exactly for what she had to expect.

"Do not get up tomorrow," he added, "until you see the sun and hear a golden bell ring. Then you will find your breakfast waiting for you here, and the horse you are to ride will be ready in the courtyard. He will also bring you back again when you come with your daughter a month hence. Farewell. Take a rose to Beauty, and remember your promise!"

The merchant was only too glad when the Beast went away, and though he could not sleep for sadness, he lay down until the sun rose. Then, after a hasty breakfast, he went to gather Beauty's rose and mounted his horse, which carried him off so swiftly that in an instant he had lost sight of the palace, and he was still wrapped in gloomy thoughts when it stopped before the door of the cottage.

His sons and daughters, who had been very uneasy at his long absence, rushed to meet him, eager to know the result of his journey, which, seeing him mounted upon a splendid horse and wrapped in a rich mantle, they supposed was favorable. He hid the truth from them at first, only saying sadly to Beauty as he gave her the rose:

"Here is what you asked me to bring; you little know what it has cost."

But this excited their curiosity so greatly that presently he told them his adventures beginning to end, and then they were all very unhappy. The girls lamented loudly over their lost hopes, and the sons declared that their father should not return to this terrible castle and began to make plans for killing the Beast if it should come to fetch him. But he reminded them that he had promised to go back. Then the girls were very angry with Beauty and said it was all her fault: if she had asked for something sensible this would never have happened. They complained bitterly that they should have to suffer for her folly.

Poor Beauty, much distressed, said to them:

"I have indeed caused this misfortune, but I assure you I did it innocently. Who could have guessed that to ask for a rose in the middle of summer would cause so much misery? But as I did the mischief, it is only just that I should suffer for it. I will therefore go back with my father to keep his promise."

At first nobody would hear of this arrangement, and her father and brothers, who loved her dearly, declared that nothing should make them let her go. But Beauty was firm. As the time drew near she divided all her little possessions between her sisters and said good-bye to everything she loved. When the fatal day came, she encouraged and cheered her father as they mounted the horse which had brought him back. It seemed to fly rather than gallop, but so smoothly that Beauty was not frightened; indeed, she would have enjoyed the journey if she had not feared what might happen to her at the end of it. Her father still tried to persuade her to go back, but in vain. While they were talking the night fell, and then, to their great surprise, wonderful colored lights began to shine in all directions, and splendid fireworks blazed out before them. All the forest was illuminated by them, and it even felt pleasantly warm, though the forest had been bitterly cold before. This lasted until they reached the avenue of orange trees, where statues were holding flaming torches. When they got nearer to the palace, they saw that it was illuminated from the roof to the ground, and music sounded softly from the courtyard. "The Beast must be very hungry," said

Beauty, trying to laugh, "if he makes all this rejoicing over the arrival of his prey."

But in spite of her anxiety, she could not help admiring all the wonderful things she saw.

The horse stopped at the foot of the flight of steps leading to the terrace, and when they dismounted, her father led her to the little room he had been in before, where they found a splendid fire burning, and the table daintily spread with a delicious supper.

The merchant knew that this was meant for them. Beauty, who was rather less frightened now that she had passed through so many rooms and had seen nothing of the Beast, was quite willing to begin, for her long ride had made her very hungry. They had hardly finished their meal when the noise of the Beast's footsteps was heard approaching, and Beauty clung to her father in terror, which became all the greater when she saw how frightened he was. But when the Beast really appeared, though she trembled at the sight of him, she made a great effort to hide her horror and saluted him respectfully.

This evidently pleased the Beast. After looking at her he said, in a tone that might have struck terror into the boldest heart, though he did not seem to be angry:

"Good evening, old man. Good evening, Beauty."

The merchant was too terrified to reply, but Beauty answered sweetly:

"Good evening, Beast."

"Have you come willingly?" asked the Beast. "Will you be content to stay here when your father goes away?"

Beauty answered bravely that she was quite prepared to stay.

"I am pleased with you," said the Beast. "As you have come of your own accord, you may stay. As for you, old man," he added, turning to the merchant, "at sunrise tomorrow you will take your departure. When the bell rings get up quickly and eat your breakfast, and you will find the same horse waiting to take you home. But remember that you must never expect to see my palace again."

Then turning to Beauty, he said:

"Take your father into the next room and help him choose everything you think your brothers and sisters would like to have. You will find two traveling trunks there; fill them as full as you can. It is only just that you should send them something very precious as a remembrance of yourself."

Then he went away, after saying

"Good-bye, Beauty; good-bye, old man"; and though Beauty was beginning to think with great dismay of her father's departure, she was afraid to disobey the Beast's orders, and they went into the next room, which had shelves and cupboards all around it. They were greatly surprised at the riches it contained. There were splendid dresses fit for a queen, with all the ornaments that were to be worn with them. When Beauty opened the cupboards, she was quite dazzled by the gorgeous jewels that lay in heaps upon every shelf. After choosing a vast quantity, which she divided between her sisters—for she had made a heap of the wonderful dresses for each of them—she opened the last chest which was full of gold.

"I think, Father," she said, "that as the gold will be more useful to you, we had better take out the other things and fill the trunks with it."

So they did this, but the more they put in, the more room there seemed to be. At last they put back all the jewels and dresses they had taken out, and Beauty even added as many more of the jewels as she could carry at once. Then the trunks still were not too full, but they were so heavy that an elephant could not have carried them!

"The Beast was mocking us," cried the merchant. "He must have pretended to give us all these things, knowing that I could not carry them away."

"Let us wait and see," said Beauty. "I cannot believe that he meant to deceive us. All we can do is to fasten them up and leave them ready."

So they did this and returned to the little room, where to their astonish-ment, they found breakfast ready. The merchant ate his with a good appetite, as the Beast's generosity made him believe that he might perhaps venture to come back soon and see Beauty. But she felt sure that her father was leaving her forever, so she was very sad when the bell rang sharply for the second time and warned them that the time had come to part. They went down into the courtyard where two horses were wait-ing, one loaded with the two trunks and the other for him to ride. They were pawing the ground in their impa-tience to start, and the merchant was forced to bid Beauty a hasty farewell. As soon as her father mounted his horse, he went off at such a pace that Beauty lost sight of him in an instant. Then she began to cry and wandered sadly back to her own room.

But she soon found that she was very sleepy, and because she had nothing better to do, she lay down and instantly fell asleep. She then dreamed that she was walking by a brook bordered with trees, and lamenting her sad fate, when a young prince, handsomer than anyone she had ever seen, and with a voice that went straight to her heart, came and said to her, "Ah, Beauty! You are not so unfortunate as you suppose. Here you will be rewarded for all you have suffered elsewhere. Your every wish shall be gratified. Only try to find me out, no matter how I may be disguised, as I love you dearly. In making me happy you will find your own happiness. Be as true hearted as you are beautiful, and we shall have nothing left to wish for."

"What can I do, Prince, to make you happy?" asked Beauty.

"Only be grateful," he answered, "and do not trust too much to your eyes. But above all, do not desert me until you have saved me from my cruel misery."

After this she dreamed she found herself in a room with a stately and beautiful lady who said to her:

"Dear Beauty, try not to regret all you have left behind you, for you are destined to a better fate. Only do not let yourself be deceived by appearances."

Beauty found her dreams so interesting that she was in no hurry to awake, but presently the clock roused her by calling her name softly twelve times. Then she got up and found her dressing table set out with everything she could possibly want. When her grooming was finished, she found dinner was waiting in the room next to hers.

But dinner does not take very long when you are all by yourself and very soon she sat down cozily in the corner of a sofa, and began to think about the charming Prince she had seen in her dream.

"He said I could make him happy," said Beauty to herself.

"It seems, then, that this horrible Beast keeps him a prisoner. How can I set him free? I wonder why they both told me not to trust appearances? I don't understand it. But, after all, it was only a dream, so why should I trouble myself about it? I had better go and find something to do to amuse myself."

So she got up and began to explore some of the many rooms of the palace.

The first she entered was lined with mirrors, and Beauty saw herself reflected on every side, and thought she had never seen such a charming room. Then a bracelet which was hanging from a chandelier caught her eye, and on taking it down she was greatly surprised to find that it held a portrait of her unknown admirer, just as she had seen him in her dream. With great delight she slipped the bracelet on her arm and went into a gallery of pictures, where she soon found a portrait of the same handsome Prince, as large as life, and so well painted that as she studied it he seemed to smile kindly at her. Tearing herself away from the portrait at last, she passed through into a room which contained every musical instrument under the sun. Here she amused herself for a long while in trying some of the instruments and singing until she was tired. The next room was a library, and she saw everything she had ever wanted to read, as well as everything she had read, and it seemed to her that a whole lifetime would not be enough even to read the names of the books, there were so many. By this time it was growing dusk, and wax candles in diamond and ruby candlesticks were beginning to light themselves in every room.

Beauty found her supper served just at the time she preferred to have it, but she did not see anyone or hear a sound, and though her father had warned her that she would be alone, she began to find it rather dull.

But she heard the Beast coming and wondered tremblingly if he meant to eat her up now.

However, he did not seem at all ferocious, and only said gruffly:

"Good evening, Beauty."

She answered cheerfully and managed to conceal her terror. Then the Beast asked her how she had been amusing herself, and she told him all the rooms she had seen.

Then he asked if she thought she could be happy in his palace, and Beauty answered that everything was so beautiful that she would be very hard to please if she could not be happy. After about an hour's talk, Beauty began to think that the Beast was not nearly so terrible as she had supposed at first. Then he got up to leave her and said in his gruff voice:

"Do you love me, Beauty? Will you marry me?"

"Oh! What shall I say?" cried Beauty, for she was afraid to make the Beast angry by refusing.

"Say 'yes' or 'no' without fear," he replied.

"Oh! No, Beast," said Beauty hastily.

"Since you will not, then good night, Beauty," he said.

And she answered, "Good night, Beast," very glad to find that her refusal had not provoked him. And after he was gone she was very soon in bed and asleep, dreaming of her unknown Prince. She thought he came and said to her:

"Ah, Beauty! Why are you so unkind to me? I fear I am fated to be unhappy for many a long day still."

And then her dreams changed, but the charming Prince figured in them all. When morning came, her first thought was to look at the portrait and see if it was really like him, and she found that it certainly was.

This morning she decided to amuse herself in the garden, for the sun shone and all the fountains were flowing. She was astonished to find the very place was familiar to her, and she came to the brook where the myrtle trees were growing, where she had first met the Prince in her dream. That made her think more than ever that he must be kept a prisoner by the Beast. When she was tired, she went back to the palace and found a new room full of material for every kind of work—ribbons to make into bows and silks to work into flowers. Then there was an aviary full of rare birds, which were so tame that they flew to Beauty as soon as they saw her and perched upon her shoulders and her head.

"Pretty little creatures," she said, "how I wish that your cage was nearer to my room, that I might often hear you sing!"

Upon saying that, Beauty opened a door and found to her delight that it led into her own room, though she had thought it was quite the other side of the palace.

There were more birds in a room farther on, with parrots and cockatoos that could talk, and they greeted Beauty by name. Indeed, she found them so entertaining that she took one or two back to her room, and they talked to her while she was at supper, after which the Beast paid her his usual visit. He asked the same question as before, and then with a gruff "good night" he took his departure, and Beauty went to bed to dream of her mysterious Prince.

The days passed swiftly in different amusements, and after a while Beauty found another strange thing in the palace, which often pleased her when she was tired of being alone. There was one room which she had not noticed particularly; it was empty, except that under each of the windows stood a very comfortable chair. The first time she had looked out of the window it had seemed to her that a black curtain prevented her from seeing anything outside. But the second time she went into the room, happening to be tired, she sat down in one of the chairs. Instantly the curtain was rolled aside, and a most amusing pantomime was acted before her. There were dances, colored lights, music, and pretty dresses; it was all so gay that Beauty was in ecstasy. After that she tried the other seven windows in turn, and there was some new and surprising entertainment to be seen from each of them, so that Beauty never could feel lonely anymore. Every evening after supper the Beast came to see her, and always before saying good night asked her in his terrible voice:

"Beauty, will you marry me?"

And it seemed to Beauty, now that she understood him better, that when she said, "No, Beast," he went away quite sad. But her happy dreams of the handsome young Prince soon made her forget the poor Beast, and the only thing that at all disturbed her was to be constantly told to distrust appearances, to let her heart guide her, and not let her eyes guide her, and many other equally perplexing things, which, consider as she would, she could not understand.

So everything went on for a long time, until at last, happy as she was, Beauty began to long for the sight of her father and her brothers and sisters. One night, seeing her look very sad, the Beast asked her what was the matter. Beauty had quite ceased to be afraid of him. Now she knew that he was really gentle despite his ferocious looks and his dreadful voice. So she answered that she was longing to see her home once more. Upon hearing this, the Beast seemed deadly distressed and cried miserably.

"Ah! Beauty, have you the heart to desert an unhappy Beast like this? What more do you want to make you happy? Is it because you hate me that you want to escape?"

"No, dear Beast," answered Beauty softly. "I do not hate you, and I should be very sorry never to see you anymore, but I long to see my father again. Only let me go for two months, and I promise to come back to you and stay for the rest of my life."

The Beast, who had been sighing dolefully while she spoke, now replied:

"I cannot refuse anything you ask, even though it could cost me my life. Take the four boxes you will find in the room next to your own and fill them with everything you wish to take with you. But remember your promise and come back when the two months are over, or you may have cause to repent it, for if you do not arrive in good time, you will find your faithful Beast dead. You will not need any chariot to bring you back. Only say good-bye to all your brothers and sisters the night before you come away. When you have gone to bed, turn this ring round upon your finger and say firmly: 'I wish to go back to my palace and see my Beast again.' Good night, Beauty. Fear nothing, sleep peacefully, and before long you shall see your father once more."

As soon as Beauty was alone she hastened to fill the boxes with all the rare and precious things she saw around her. Only when she was tired of heaping things into them did the boxes seem to be full.

Then she went to bed, but could hardly sleep for joy. And when at last she did begin to dream of her beloved Prince, she was grieved to see him stretched upon a grassy bank sad and weary, hardly like himself.

"What is the matter?" she cried.

But he looked reproachfully at her and said, "How can you ask me, cruel one? Are you not leaving me to my death perhaps?"

"Ah! Don't be so sorrowful," cried Beauty. "I am only going to assure my father that I am safe and happy. I have promised the Beast faithfully that I will come back, and he would die of grief if I did not keep my word!"

"What would that matter to you?" said the Prince. "Surely you would not care?"

"Indeed I should be ungrateful if I did not care for such a kind Beast," cried Beauty indignantly. "I would die to save him from pain. I assure you it is not his fault that he is so ugly."

Just then a strange sound woke her—someone was speaking not very far away. Opening her eyes, she found herself in a room she had never seen before, which was certainly not nearly so splendid as those she was used to in the Beast's palace. Where could she be?

She got up and dressed hastily, and then saw that the boxes she had packed the night before were all in the room. While she was wondering by what magic the Beast had transported them and herself to this strange place, she suddenly heard her father's voice and rushed out and greeted him joyfully. Her brothers and sisters were all astonished at her appearance; as they had never expected to see her again, and there was no end to the questions they asked her. She had also much to hear about her father's journey home and what had happened to them while she was away. But when they heard that she had only come to be with them for a short time, and then must go back to the Beast's palace forever, they lamented loudly. Then Beauty asked her father what he thought could be the meaning of her strange dreams, and why the Prince constantly begged her not to

trust appearances. After much consideration he answered:

"You tell me yourself that the Beast, frightful as he is, loves you dearly, and deserves your love and gratitude for his gentleness and kindness. I think the Prince must mean for you to understand that you ought to reward him by doing as he wishes you to, in spite of his ugliness."

Beauty could not help seeing that this seemed very probable. Still, when she thought of her dear Prince who was so handsome, she did not feel at all inclined to marry the Beast. At any rate, for two months she need not decide, but could enjoy herself with her sisters. Though they were rich now and lived in a town again, with plenty of acquaintances, Beauty found that nothing amused her very much. She often thought of the palace, where she was so happy. At home she never once dreamed

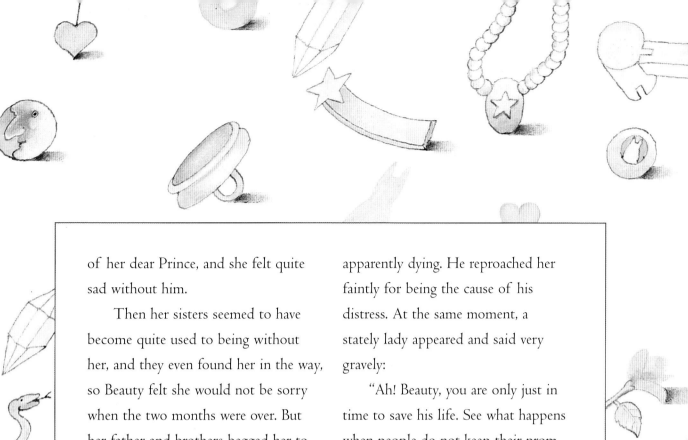

of her dear Prince, and she felt quite sad without him.

Then her sisters seemed to have become quite used to being without her, and they even found her in the way, so Beauty felt she would not be sorry when the two months were over. But her father and brothers begged her to stay and seemed so grieved at the thought of her departure, that she did not have the courage to say good-bye to them. Every day when she got up she meant to say it at night, and when night came she put if off again, until at last she had a dismal dream which helped her to make up her mind. She thought she was wandering on a lonely path in the palace gardens, when she heard groans which seemed to come from some bushes hiding the entrance of a cave, and running quickly to see what could be the matter, she found the Beast stretched out upon his side,

apparently dying. He reproached her faintly for being the cause of his distress. At the same moment, a stately lady appeared and said very gravely:

"Ah! Beauty, you are only just in time to save his life. See what happens when people do not keep their promises! If you had delayed one day more, you would have found him dead."

Beauty was so terrified by this dream that the next morning she announced her intention of going back at once, and that very night she said good-bye to her father and all her brothers and sisters. As soon as she was in bed, she turned her ring round upon her finger and said firmly:

"I wish to go back to my palace and see my Beast again," as she had been told to do.

Then she fell asleep instantly and woke up to hear the clock saying, "Beauty, Beauty," twelve times in its musical voice, which told her at once that she was really in the palace once more. Everything was just as before, and her birds were so glad to see her! But Beauty thought she had never known such a long day, for she was so anxious to see the Beast again that she felt as if supper time should never come.

But when it did come and no Beast appeared, she was really frightened. After listening and waiting for a long time, she ran down into the garden to search for him. Up and down the paths and avenues ran poor Beauty, calling him in vain, for no one answered and not a trace of him could she find, until at last, quite tired, she stopped for a minute's rest and saw that she was standing opposite the shady path she had seen in her dream. She rushed down it, and, sure enough, there was the cave and in it lay the Beast—asleep, as Beauty thought. Quite glad to have found him, she ran up and stroked his head, but to her horror he did not move or open his eyes.

"Oh! He is dead, and it is all my fault," said Beauty, crying bitterly.

But then, looking at him again, she fancied he still breathed. Hastily fetching some water from the nearest fountain, she sprinkled it over his face, and to her great delight he began to revive.

"Oh! Beast, how you frightened me!" she cried. "I never knew how much I loved you until just now, when I feared I was too late to save your life."

"Can you really love such an ugly creature as I am?" asked the Beast faintly. "Ah! Beauty, you came just in time. I was dying because I thought you had forgotten your promise. But go back now and rest, I shall see you again by and by."

Beauty, who had half expected that he would be angry with her, was reassured by his gentle voice and went back to the palace, where supper was awaiting her. Afterwards the Beast came in as usual and talked about the time she had spent with her father, asking if she had enjoyed herself and if they all had been very glad to see her.

Beauty answered politely and quite enjoyed telling him all that had happened to her. And when at last the time came for him to go, he asked the question that he had so often asked before:

"Beauty, will you marry me?"

She answered softly, "Yes, dear Beast."

As she spoke, a blaze of light sprang up before the windows of the palace, fireworks crackled and guns banged. Across the avenue of orange trees, in letters all made of fireflies, was written: "Long live the Prince and his beautiful bride."

Turning to ask the Beast what it could all mean, Beauty found that he had disappeared, and in his place stood her long-loved Prince! At the same moment the heels of a chariot were heard upon the terrace, and two ladies entered the room. One of them Beauty recognized as the stately lady she had seen in her dreams; the other was also so grand and queenly that Beauty hardly knew which to greet first.

But the one she already knew said to her companion:

"Well, Queen, this is Beauty, who has had the courage to rescue your son from the terrible enchantment. They love one another, and only your consent to their marriage is needed to make them perfectly happy."

"I consent with all my heart," cried the Queen. "How can I ever thank you enough, charming girl, for having restored my dear son to his natural form?"

And then she tenderly embraced Beauty and the Prince, who had meanwhile been greeting the Fairy and receiving her congratulations.

"Now," said the Fairy to Beauty, "I suppose you would like me to send for all your brothers and sisters to dance at your wedding?"

And so she did, and the marriage was celebrated the very next day with the utmost splendor, and Beauty and the Prince lived happily ever after.